THE
KING'S
CHRISTMAS LIST

To my beloved wife, Kristen Joy, who has always believed in me.

Published in Nashville, Tennessee, by Tommy Nelson®. Tommy Nelson is a registered trademark of Thomas Nelson, Inc.

Published in association with the Books & Such Literary Agency, Janet Kobobel Grant, 52 Mission Circle, Suite 122, PMB 170, Santa Rosa, CA 95409-5370, www.booksandsuch.biz

Thomas Nelson, Inc., titles may be purchased in bulk for educational, business, fund-raising, or sales promotional use. For information, please e-mail SpecialMarkets@ThomasNelson.com.

Unless otherwise noted, Scripture quotations are taken from *Holy Bible*, New Living Translation. © 1996. Used by permission of Tyndale House Publishers, Inc., Wheaton, Illinois 60189. All rights reserved.

Library of Congress Control Number: 2010017282

ISBN 978-1-4003-1645-8

Mfr: Hung Hing/Shenzhen, China/August, 2010/PO# 108317

THE
KING'S
CHRISTMAS LIST

by Eldon Johnson

illustrated by Bonnie Leick

NELSON

A Division of Thomas Nelson Publishers

NASHVILLE   DALLAS   MEXICO CITY   RIO DE JANEIRO

When Emma's daddy built the playhouse, an amazing thing happened. Because, you see, sometimes, when a parent's love is woven into the wood and paint of a playhouse—and then mixed just right with a child's imagination—a door is opened!

It's a door to a world known simply as "The Kingdom."

It all began for Emma and her dog, Shu-Shu, when they were decorating the playhouse for Christmas. Suddenly, Emma heard a voice behind her: "How did you make the mailbox shine like the Christmas star?"

Before Emma could even wonder about the voice, she turned around—and, sure enough, the mailbox was glowing!

Emma raced to the mailbox, but she was afraid to touch it. Finally, she looked inside. A flash of dazzling light hit her, and she saw a beautiful, golden letter!

Emma tore open the envelope. "It's an invitation from the King!" she told Shu-Shu. "It says, 'To the Honorable Lady Emma and the Gentle Dog Shu-Shu, you are hereby invited to the King's birthday party—His royal Christmas celebration!'"

Shu-Shu excitedly shouted, or barked, "We're going to meet the King!"

Emma suddenly realized her puppy was speaking. "Wait one minute! Shu-Shu, you can talk?"

"No," he replied. "It's just that now you can finally understand me!"

"This is all so strange," Emma said, looking at the invitation. "The King has invited us to His birthday party. . . . We need to give Him a present! But what can we give a king?"

Shu-Shu said, "Come on, we can find something in the playhouse!"

Back inside, Emma saw the special Christmas cake she had made with her mom. "What about the cake?"

"That's a great idea. But it looks delicious. Don't you want to eat it?" asked Shu-Shu.

Emma—still getting used to talking to a dog—said, "Well, yes, but I'd rather give it to the King. The cake is special because we made it, and the King will love it!"

Just then, they heard a voice announce: "A carriage sent from the King—for Lady Emma and the Gentle Dog Shu-Shu!"

"The King's carriage is here for *us*!" Shu-Shu barked in amazement.

Emma said, "Hurry, Shu, let's go!" She grabbed her new Christmas cape and, of course, Cherry-Bear—she didn't go anywhere without Cherry-Bear.

As they climbed into the beautiful carriage, Emma stared in wonder. "It's like a whole new world has appeared!" she exclaimed.

The horse whinnied, "Welcome, my friends. Hold on tight!"

And with that, they set off on their
adventure. A new world opened up
before them as the playhouse disappeared
behind them. They could see mountains rising along
the road in the distance.

The air was cold and deliciously fresh. Emma and Shu-Shu were snuggled in the carriage when it suddenly screeched to a halt. Emma looked down to see what made them stop.

There, trying to cross the road, was an old woman with her arm around a young boy who was shivering in the cold.

"Oh, please, pardon us," said the woman. "My grandson is very cold. I am trying to find someplace where he will be warm."

Emma felt terrible seeing the poor boy shivering on this cold, winter day.

"It's all right, ma'am," said the horse. "But we've got to go now. We're off to the King's castle!"

Emma blurted out, "Wait! Before we go, please take my Christmas cape—it will keep your grandson warm. And . . ." Emma looked at her beautiful cake, the one she wanted to give to the King. But the woman and the boy looked so hungry.

"Please take this cake too. You both need something to eat."

"Oh, no," said the grandma. "We couldn't do that. . . ."

Emma nodded and said, "I insist!" And Shu-Shu barked, "Yes, take them."

With that, Emma climbed down and handed the cake to the woman. Then she wrapped the Christmas cape around the little boy's shoulders. The boy looked so much warmer, and seeing the delicious cake, he said, "Thank you, Emma!"

As the horse bolted toward the castle, Emma wondered, *How did he know my name?*

As the countryside flew by, they came to a bridge over a rushing river, and Emma heard a child crying. "Where is that coming from?" she asked.

"It sounds like it's coming from the bridge," Shu-Shu barked.

"Oh no!" Emma said, "Let's stop and see if we can help!"

The pair climbed down from the carriage and walked to the bridge.

A mother and father were trying to comfort their daughter.
When they saw Emma and Shu-Shu, they said,
"Her teddy bear fell into the river, and it's gone!"

"Oh, no!" Emma put her arm around the girl. She was younger than Emma, and her clothes were old and worn. That bear was probably her only toy.

Emma cringed inside. She felt that she should give the girl her Cherry-Bear . . . but how could she? Cherry-Bear was her favorite toy!

"It will be okay . . . because . . ." She made up her mind and said, "Because I need you to take care of my Cherry-Bear. Can you do that for me?"

The little girl smiled. "Yes, I think I can."

Emma said, "Shu-Shu, run and get Cherry-Bear!"

Shu-Shu barked an eager yes. He darted for the carriage, excited to be able to help.

When they left, the little girl was holding Cherry-Bear close. As the carriage pulled away, the family waved and said, "Thank you, Emma and Shu-Shu!"

This time Emma said, "Shu! How did they know our names?"

Finally, they arrived at the castle. Emma and Shu-Shu thanked the horse and walked up to the grand doors—which opened all by themselves! As they walked in, the court announcer said, "Welcome, Lady Emma and her Honorable Gentle Dog Shu-Shu!"

They were still shaking hands when a fanfare of trumpets shook the room:

"HEAR YE! HEAR YE!
All hail the High King!
Let the royal
Christmas celebration
begin!"

Then, the King entered in His shining Christmas robes! Emma and Shu-Shu stared at Him in amazement.

As He took His throne for His birthday party, something odd happened—all the guests started giving gifts to each other, but no one gave a gift to the King.

"This is the strangest birthday party ever," Emma said.

"Yeah, even I get gifts on my birthday, and I'm just a pup!" Shu-Shu barked. "Come on, let's ask the King."

"Shu-Shu!" Emma tried to stop the little dog, but all she could do was run after him.

The King seemed to expect them and said, "Welcome, Lady Emma and the Honorable Shu-Shu. I understand you have a question for Me?"

Emma looked up and said, "We see everyone giving gifts to each other. But Christmas is Your birthday, and this is Your party."

Then she looked deeply into His eyes and asked, "Why isn't anyone giving You a gift? Is it different for a King?"

"Well, now," began the King, "it is a little different—and that's the reason I invited you here today."

"Really?" Emma asked.

"Yes. You see, because Christmas is such a special day, people celebrate by giving lots of gifts. But over the years, people got so busy giving gifts to each other that they forgot that I, too, love a Christmas gift given from the heart!"

The whole crowd was listening as Emma said, "Oh, King, we had a gift for You! We brought You a cake, but . . ."

The King stopped her. "I know, My dear Emma." And with a wave of His hand, the family and the grandmother and her grandson appeared, clothed in glowing white!

Emma gasped in surprise. "Are they angels?" she asked.

"Yes," the King smiled. "I sent them out to look for the true spirit of Christmas, and they found it in you!"

The King lifted Emma up on His knee and said, "You see, by sharing your favorite things with them, you showed My people how to give Me a Christmas gift.

"For I do have a Christmas list, but many have forgotten it."

His voice echoed throughout the hall—

"Anyone who desires to give Me a gift, behold!
Give food to the hungry and clothes to the cold,
Give care to the poor, both young and old,
Whatever gift you've given to a person in need,
Is indeed a gift you have given to Me."

Emma said, "You mean, by giving to others we are actually giving You a present?"

"That's right," the King said with the greatest of smiles.

He continued, "My precious child, it takes a lot of love and courage to share the things that are dear to you. When you stopped to help others on your way to the castle today, you showed them what My love looks like."

The King opened His arms wide for a great big hug. "And My love for them—and for you—is so big, it's the greatest Christmas present of all."

THE END

But it's really just the beginning!
The rest of the story is up to you—just turn the page.

Give a Gift to the King!

"'When did we ever see you hungry and feed you? . . .
When did we ever see you sick or in prison and visit you?' . . .
And the King will say, 'I tell you the truth, when you did it to one of the least of these my brothers and sisters, you were doing it to me!'"

Matthew 25:37–40

Log on to www.TheKingsAdventure.com to find out how you can give a birthday gift to the King of Kings this Christmas! There you will find lots of ideas to help people in need. Plus there are links to amazing opportunities to give through trusted names such as World Vision and Blood:Water Mission.

Start your own adventure of giving and changing lives!

$0=
CHRISTMAS **CAROLING**
FOR **CANNED GOODS**
THAT WILL STOCK
YOUR LOCAL FOOD PANTRY

$1=
ONE**YEAR**
OF**WATER**
FOR AN **AFRICAN**
FOR MORE INFORMATION VISIT: **BLOODWATERMISSION.COM**

🩸 blood:water mission

$25=
TWO **CHICKENS**
THAT GIVE **FOOD** & **INCOME**
FOR **FAMILIES**

World Vision